CHAPTER 1

SEE YA, EARTH!

I've been thinking about moving to another planet. I'm half serious about it, too. I know it sounds kind of silly, and probably impossible. But I'd like to hop on the next spacecraft and leave this place.

It's not that I don't like Earth. I like it a lot! (I've only lived here all my life.) There are so many things I like about Earth, like for instance:

THE OCEANS

SUSHI

MY UKULELE

MAC AND CHEESE WITH PICKLES

CHOCOLATE AND SWEETS

AIR
(I DO LIKE TO BREATHE)

COMIC BOOKS

WATER
(ALSO KNOWN AS H_2O)

BABIES

And so many things I would miss!

TREES

ICE CREAM
(LOTS OF FOOD ON THIS LIST, I REALIZE)

ROCKS AND SHELLS

MY BED

MY FRIEND **RITA**,
THE FRENCH-SPEAKING SPIDER

AND BASICALLY

ALL ANIMALS,

BIG AND SMALL

The list could go on and on. I can't believe I didn't mention bubble bath, gel pens, beetles, movie nights, Play-Doh, hot baths, computers, microscopes, Halloween, and my pyjamas!

… and my bike. Sorry, bike. I just hate drawing bikes, but I DO love you, bike.

As I said, Earth itself is fine. It's all the humans who live on it that I'd like to avoid.

Humans are EVERYWHERE on Earth, and they can be extremely annoying.

COMMON HUMAN

(MALE VERSION. BUT I'M NOT SEXIST; THE FEMALE VERSION IS JUST AS WEIRD.)

RANDOM TUFTS OF HAIR HERE AND THERE, FOR NO GOOD REASON

THINK THEY'RE KINGS OF THE PLANET

BAD BREATH

I LOVE BEER

RIDICULOUS BELLY BUTTON

UGLY TOES AND SMELLY FEET

TENDENCY TO THROW RUBBISH EVERYWHERE

I MEAN, EWW, RIGHT?

Look, I know that humans do a lot of great things, such as music, or comic books, or pasta. But really, what they do a lot more is fight and destroy the planet.

OTHER THINGS HUMANS DO

THAT I DON'T LIKE:

STEP ON **BUGS** FOR **FUN**

"FORGET" TO PICK UP THEIR DOG'S POO

MAKE FUN OF PEOPLE WITH **DIFFERENT** BODY SHAPES OR SKIN COLOUR

STAND **TOO CLOSE** TO ME, OR EVEN **WORSE**, PAT MY HEAD

Not ALL of them are annoying, of course. Some are nice, like:

Both are caring and helpful people who I can't imagine would ever throw their rubbish in the woods. And I am nice too, even though I'm a human being as far as I know (but I might also be a robot built and programmed by a mad scientist).

But I've had enough of the rest of them, especially since I met my very best friend for ever...

Meh is this extremely awesome creature I discovered a month ago in my rubbish bin. She's round and pink and soft and smelly and utterly ADORABLE.

I did lots of research, but I couldn't find the name of the species she belonged to, so I worked out that I had discovered a new animal. Not many new animal species are discovered nowadays except for bugs and microbes, so it was a pretty big deal for a young scientist like me.

I decided to name the species

OLGAMUS RIDICULUS,

after myself, and I think it sounds terrific.

Meh is the best thing that's ever happened to me!

I won't describe Meh too much here because I already spent a whole other notebook studying her, but here's a quick summary:

RANDOM INFORMATION ABOUT MEH:

She sleeps in a rubbish bin.

She's cuddly.

She only eats olives.

She says "meh" all the time, except when she's excited—
then she says:

Up close, she looks super scary, like Jaws.

She's easy to draw from all sides: up, down, front, side.

And here are new things I've worked out about her since then:

SHE LIKES HER **OLIVES** BETTER IF I SERVE THEM IN A **FANCY CRYSTAL BOWL.**

AHEM. HELLO!

EVERY TIME I GO TO THE **TOILET,** SHE WATCHES ME WITH AN **INTENSE** LOOK ON HER FACE.

MEH!

SHE CAN'T STAND IT WHEN I TALK ON THE **PHONE** OR PLAY ON MY **COMPUTER.**

IF YOU PUT **SUNGLASSES** ON HER **BEHIND,** IT MAKES A REALLY **FUNNY FACE.**

Meh is so special (and weird) that I'm pretty sure she comes from another planet. Since there are no other known Olgamus specimens on Earth, I wonder: where do her parents come from?

She *could* be a mix of two existing Earth creatures, like a pig and a capybara*, but I seriously doubt it.

*CAPYBARA: GIANT GUINEA-PIG-LIKE **RODENT** FROM SOUTH AMERICA.

2
WHERE IS
MEH FROM?

Meh is way too peculiar to be from Earth. My alien theory is the one I like best.

I HAVE AN IDEA!

Meh and I will move to another planet. I can take her back where she came from, and then I'll stay there and keep her company for ever. I will get to meet her family, her friends, and her tribe if she has one. That would be

AWESOME.

Can you imagine a planet without any humans, just Olgamuses?

I can. It would be THE BEST PLANET EVER. Although a bit smelly, if I am judging by the only Olgamus I know.

I would bring a hammock and live there among all the Olgamuses, like Jane Goodall with her chimp friends. I would learn how to communicate with them; I would play them ukulele songs; I would teach them human things.

Here are some of the tricks I would show them:

HOW TO CHOREOGRAPH **THE BEST DANCE MOVES**

HOW TO MAKE **MAC AND CHEESE** WITH **PICKLES**

IT'S DELICIOUS, OLGAMUS #863!

HOW TO **READ**

HOW TO **BURP** THE ALPHABET

ABCDEFGHiJKLⁿⁿ...

Like any great biologist, I would bring a notebook to record my findings, of course. I already have a number of research questions that, so far, haven't been answered:

1. DO OLGAMUSES HATCH FROM EGGS?

2. DO THEY HAVE NATURAL ENEMIES OR PREDATORS ON THEIR PLANET?

3. DO THEY HAVE THEIR OWN LANGUAGE? MINE ONLY SAYS "MEH" ALL THE TIME (AND "RUBBER" WHEN SHE BURPS).

4. ARE THEY **AMPHIBIANS?**

5. DO THEY HAVE **SPECIAL SKILLS,**
LIKE SEEING IN THE DARK OR BUILDING NESTS?

6. DO THEY LIVE IN **GROUPS,**
AND DO THEY HAVE A **LEADER?**

It would be fantastic. Of course, I would also explore their planet. I'm sure it's a very awesome and interesting place. Here's how I imagine it:

One thing I know for sure: there must be olive trees on Meh's planet, because olives are the only thing she eats. Her planet probably has beautiful olive trees EVERYWHERE! Maybe it looks like Greece, which I found out is totally gorgeous.

GREECE
(IN MY
IMAGINATION)

Of course, if I *did* move to another planet, I'd miss some people from Earth. I would miss my pet spider, Rita, who lives under my sink and speaks French. Or maybe I could take her with me.

NOTE TO SELF:

MAKE SURE SPIDERS CAN TRAVEL IN SPACE.

ALSO: DO THEY MAKE SPACE SUITS IN SPIDER SIZES?

Would I miss any humans? Perhaps. The one I'd miss the most would be my friend Chuck.

Chuck always hangs out at the dog park. I like the dog park too, so I put away my plans to travel into space, and put a lead on Meh, and we go off to the dog park.

Chuck is there, of course, surrounded by dozens of dogs. I tell him about my plans, hoping he'll want to join us on the trip.

Chuck is good at making human friends. Much better than I am. Even his dog, Mister, the ugliest canine specimen in the whole universe, has lots of friends.

flashback

Chuck and I became friends the day Mister peed on Meh. We all started hanging out after that; Meh and Mister also became great buddies, running around the park like maniacs, smelling each other's behinds and licking each other's faces.

FUNNY-LOOKING CREATURES OF THE WORLD, UNITE!

34

Chuck was right to ask. This idea of mine was probably pure fantasy. It wouldn't be the first time I'd been called a dreamer.

But hey, many scientists before me were thought of as crazy before they changed the world, right?

LIKE:

GALILEO

IN 1610, HE BELIEVED THAT **THE EARTH** WAS ORBITING **AROUND THE SUN.**

LUDWIG BOLTZMANN

IN 1880 HE **TRIED** TO CONVINCE THE WORLD THAT **ATOMS** AND **MOLECULES** EXISTED.

ROBERT GODDARD

IN 1919, HE BELIEVED IT WAS **POSSIBLE** TO SEND A **ROCKET** TO THE **MOON.**

It was time to do what I do best:

3

I'M ON TOP OF IT

The easiest place to find info about space travel would be right here at home on the internet, but I felt like going to the library because I have a human friend there: Ms Swoop. She's the best librarian ever, and she helped me find Meh about a month ago when I'd lost her, so I like to stop by and say hello from time to time.

MS SWOOP

IT'S HER

SHE'S AWESOME

Also, I have to admit that I go mostly because I really like to check out comic books. I'm a big comic book fan! Life is not worth living when I don't have good comic books around.

I took a sniff, and it was true: although Meh always
smells like a mixture of week-old rubbish and eggs,
today was worse. I'd got used to the smell by now,
but I could understand Ms Swoop's concern.

WHAT ARE YOU TWO UP TO TODAY?

WELL, I'VE BEEN THINKING OF MOVING TO ANOTHER PLANET. I'M **TIRED** OF THIS ONE.

TELL ME ABOUT IT. I **WISH** I COULD GO WITH YOU. WHICH PLANET DO YOU HAVE IN MIND?

I'M TRYING TO FIND **MEH'S PLANET.** YOU KNOW, WHERE SHE COMES FROM.

GOOD PLAN! LET'S SEE WHAT WE HAVE ABOUT **SPACE TRAVEL.**

40

We found a dozen books, and I sat down at my favourite table next to the window.

HERE'S WHAT
I FOUND OUT:

OK, bad news. Humans HAVE travelled to space, but no human being has made it to another planet. The furthest we've been is to the moon. (Apparently, further than that is dangerous. Scientists prefer to send probes and robots.)

SOME LUCKY ROBOTS!

SAYONARA!

But they ARE working on it, so all hope's not lost. Science moves quickly. Thirty years ago, nobody knew we would have smartphones by now. Who knows where it could lead us in a couple of years?

I'm still hoping for

Guess what: a lot of women have been to

SPACE!

VALENTINA TERESHKOVA:
FIRST WOMAN IN SPACE, 1963

SALLY RIDE:
FIRST AMERICAN WOMAN
IN SPACE, 1983

SVETLANA SAVITSKAYA:
FIRST WOMAN TO PERFORM
A SPACEWALK, 1984 (HOW
COOL IS THAT? I WANT TO
PERFORM A SPACEWALK)

MAE JEMISON:
FIRST AFRICAN
AMERICAN WOMAN
IN SPACE, 1993

EILEEN COLLINS:
FIRST WOMAN
SHUTTLE PILOT
AND SHUTTLE
COMMANDER, 1995

OLGA:
FIRST GIRL TO LIVE ON
ANOTHER PLANET

MEH: FIRST OLGAMUS
TO ACCOMPANY A
HUMAN INTO SPACE

ACCORDING TO THESE BOOKS, PEOPLE DON'T GET TO SPACE BY SITTING AROUND WITH THEIR FINGERS UP THEIR NOSES. THEY NEED TO WORK HARD AT MATHS, PHYSICS, AND ASTRONOMY. I'M ON TOP OF IT.

"Any luck?" asked Ms Swoop.

"Not really," I said. I explained about the limits of space travel.

I thanked Ms Swoop, took a few books out of the library, put Meh back into my backpack, and went home.

I put Meh to bed in her little rubbish bin, gave her two olives as her bedtime snack, and sat down in my lab. I had some studying to do.

4

THE MUSEUM OF
WEIRD FOODS

Meh's been sleeping for twelve hours and won't wake up. That's lucky, since it gives me more time to study. So far I've discovered some pretty cool stuff about space.

SPACE FACTS:

THERE IS A PLANET MADE **ENTIRELY** OF **DIAMONDS!**

SPACE IS COMPLETELY **SILENT** (SO MUCH FOR MY UKULELE PLAYING).

SATURN HAS **62** MOONS.

PFF!

I HAVE ONLY ONE, BUT IT'S THE BEST.

THERE ARE GIANT POOLS
OF **WATER**
FLOATING IN SPACE.

IF YOU EVER STEPPED ON THE **MOON,**
YOUR FOOTPRINTS WOULD PROBABLY
STAY THERE **FOR EVER.**

MY
FOOTPRINT
4 EVER!

THERE ARE MORE THAN **500,000** PIECES
OF **SPACE JUNK** IN THE EARTH'S ORBIT.
(HUMANS! DO WE HAVE TO
POLLUTE **EVERYTHING?**)

Interesting, huh? After a while, I got hungry, but there was nothing in the fridge.

OBSERVATION # 2:

BRILLIANT SCIENTISTS OFTEN NEGLECT THEIR BASIC HUMAN NEEDS WHILE STUDYING.

I woke up Meh, and we took off to the shop.

My favourite place to buy food is the corner shop, STUFF 'N' THINGS 'N' MORE!

The owner there, Mr Hoopah, is another one of my human friends.

FIG. 4: MR HOOPAH

HOW ARE YOU DOING, FAVOURITE LOYAL CUSTOMER?

EXTREMELY WELCOMING AND POLITE

EXTREMELY ELEGANT & HAIRY

EXTREMELY SHINY SHIRT

I told him all about my plans to travel to another planet. He was sad that I wanted to leave but relieved when I told him I can't, because let's face it: I'm one of his best customers.

So I took some time to shop around. STUFF 'N' THINGS 'N' MORE is like a museum of weird products, and I could spend my life in there. Just look at these new finds:

It probably all sounds weird, and you might ask why anybody would want to buy food there in the first place. Well, I can think of

3 REASONS.

Reason #1: I'm a scientific person, and my curious brain makes me want to try out new things.

LET'S EAT **GRASS** AND SEE IF IT'S ANY GOOD!

Reason #2: Mr Hoopah is an awfully nice man, and truly nice humans are so rare that I feel like showing him my appreciation.

Reason #3: I've actually discovered delicious stuff in his shop in the past, like wasabi ice cream or his special homemade popcorn that comes in 99 different flavours.

STUFF 'N' THINGS 'N' MORE doesn't just sell food! It also has everyday stuff for around the house, like:

DANDELION-GROWING KITS

T-REX-SHAPED TOILET BRUSHES

TOE EXERCISERS

FOR STRONG, THIN AND FIT **TOES!**

CHAMPAGNE–SHAPED
MILK BOTTLES FOR **BABIES**

VERY OLD **VIDEO GAMES** THAT NOBODY EVER WANTS

SLOTH FIGHT!

SLUG RACE!

Another thing I like about this shop is that Mr Hoopah always has a treat for Meh and me, like he did today.

"Look, beloved customer," said Mr Hoopah. "I set these aside for your beautiful pet. They are a very rare, delicious importation from Finland."

Meh is a real olive gourmet, so I took them and thanked Mr Hoopah. Then he gave me a spaghetti-and-meatball-flavoured lollipop, and we said goodbye.

As I left the shop, I found myself face-to-face with the Lalas.

For those of you who haven't read my first book, the Lalas are two human specimens who I often find particularly annoying. They've been making fun of me since we were babies, so I would normally put them in the "horrible humans" category. They also kidnapped Meh once and gave her a beauty makeover. However, they did help me with my Olgamus research, so I have since moved them to the "mildly annoying" category.

FIG. 5: THE LALAS

BOTH PAINFULLY **PRETTY**

SMELL LIKE **VANILLA** ALL THE TIME

ALWAYS DRESSED **FASHIONABLY**

OBSESSED WITH POP STARS

BIP BIBOP

ALWAYS WORKING HARD TO BE **CUTE**

ANNOYINGNESS LEVEL TODAY: MEDIUM

HEY, OLGA! HOW'S OUR LOVELY LITTLE FRIEND?

OMG! SHE LOOKS **TERRIBLE!** LOOK AT THE CIRCLES UNDER HER EYES! YOU'RE NEGLECTING HER. DIDN'T YOU FOLLOW **EVEN ONE** OF OUR BEAUTY TIPS?

AND THE **SMELL!** IT'S WORSE THAN EVER! MEH! YOU ARE WAY OVERDUE FOR A **MAKEOVER!**

DO YOU GUYS CARE ABOUT ANYTHING BESIDES **BEAUTY?** MEH IS **PERFECT** THE WAY SHE IS.

I still hadn't eaten yet, and

OBSERVATION # 3:

WHEN I'M HUNGRY I CAN BE SUPER GROUCHY, SO I PICKED MEH UP AND LEFT.

I know the Lalas are only trying to be nice, but they always criticize other people's appearances. I call that kind of behaviour a "horrible human" habit.

Still, I gave Meh a bath after we'd eaten our breakfast, just in case. I had to admit the smell was getting worse.

SHE LOVES BATHS!!!!

I BATHE HER IN MY **BIG PASTA POT**

HER FAVOURITE **BATH TOYS**

While Meh was taking her nap, I had time to think. If Meh came from another planet, there was a good chance there were other creatures out there too. Was I ready to meet them?

There was nothing about them in my books, so I guessed the internet was going to be my best bet. You won't believe what I found out.

5

ALIEN ENCOUNTERS

If I'm to encounter space creatures other than Olgamuses, I'd like it much better if they were friendly. But do aliens even exist?

Based on my research, there is no proof that aliens have ever been present on Earth (except for Meh, of course, if she is one). But a lot of humans through the ages have claimed to have had encounters with creatures from space.

Here are some real aliens that people have met on Earth:

THE FLATWOODS MONSTERS: TALL HUMANOID WITH A **SPADE-SHAPED HEAD.**

THE GREYS: GREY-SKINNED HUMANOIDS, USUALLY THREE TO FOUR FEET TALL, **BALD,** WITH BLACK ALMOND-SHAPED EYES, NOSTRILS **WITHOUT A NOSE,** SLITS FOR MOUTHS, **NO EARS** AND THREE TO FOUR FINGERS INCLUDING THUMB.

THE HOPKINSVILLE GOBLINS: SMALL, **GREENISH-SILVER** HUMANOIDS.

THE LITTLE GREEN MEN: DIMINUTIVE **GREEN HUMANOIDS**

THE NORDIC ALIENS (OR SPACE BROTHERS): TALL AND BLOND WITH **BLUE EYES.**

OBSERVATION #4:

NONE OF THEM ARE AS CUTE AS MEH.

This is extremely disappointing. *Humanoid* means "resembling a human being." Seriously, would I waste my time travelling to space if it was only to meet humanlike creatures (who might be ten times more evil than actual humans)?

I was hoping to meet interesting beings like

THESE:

I was interrupted from my research by a horrifying noise. It sounded like a defective vacuum cleaner trying to suck up a bathtubful of jelly.

I ran to the bedroom, where I found Meh puking all over my best dress. Half-digested olives were spewed everywhere. It was gross.

She looked at me with the most miserable eyes you've ever seen. The Lalas were right. She DID look awful.

I went to get the jar of peanut-butter-filled olives, which I found empty. The expiration date hadn't passed—it was a few weeks away. But I have to say that just the thought of this strange food made me a bit queasy myself. I threw it in the recycling and made a note:

OBSERVATION # 5:

MEH CAN'T DIGEST PEANUT-BUTTER-FILLED OLIVES. MAYBE SHE'S ALLERGIC TO PEANUT BUTTER? INVESTIGATE FURTHER.

I cleaned up Meh's mess, gave her a bath (again), and sat down with her. We cuddled and watched a movie together. That's what I feel like doing when I'm sick, so I guessed it would make Meh feel better too.

We watched my favourite movie ever, *E.T.*

E.T. is the story of an alien who gets stranded on Earth when his spaceship leaves without him. A young boy named Elliot befriends him, and E.T. becomes part of the family. But then some really evil scientists want to capture the alien to observe him.

These scientists are so scary! Why can't they just observe creatures gently, like the boy in the movie, or like me? Pfft, humans.

OBSERVATION # 6:

SOME SCIENTISTS CAN BE EVIL. THIS COMES AS A SHOCK.

I WILL **NEVER** STUDY YOU AGAINST YOUR WILL, MEH.

Meh burped softly and fell asleep in my arms. I stayed awake for a long time, stroking her fur, making sure she didn't get sick again.

REAL LOVE IS...

WHEN YOU DON'T CARE ABOUT YOUR BEST FRIEND'S BURPS

6

WHAT ABOUT SPIDERS?

In the morning when I got up, Meh was still asleep. I let her sleep in. When she woke up, I fed her a big bowl of ordinary olives, no peanut butter. She wolfed it down in her normal way, like a starved seagull, almost choking on every bite.

OBSERVATION # 7:

MEH'S NORMAL DIGESTION PROCESS: NO CHEWING, STRAIGHT TO POO.

I thought that she'd like to take a walk to the dog park, see her friend, Mister, and breathe some fresh air, but when I put a lead on her, she wouldn't move a muscle. (Do Olgamuses have muscles?)

OK, MEH, WHAT'S UP? ARE YOU **STILL TIRED?**

I didn't feel like spending the day alone watching Meh sleep, so I called Chuck and asked him if he wanted to come over to my place. Maybe Meh didn't need the company, but I sure did.

Chuck arrived with a bag of homemade marshmallow-and-chocolate cookies that tasted so delicious, it made me reconsider my trip to space.

OBSERVATION #8:

THERE IS NO GUARANTEE

THAT I'LL FIND COOKIES ON ANOTHER PLANET

(SO I MIGHT AS WELL STUFF MY FACE NOW).

Chuck and I weren't sick, so we ate the entire bag of cookies in 3 minutes, 53 seconds exactly. They were delicious.

"So," Chuck said. "What's up with your space travel plans?" I explained that it wasn't going to be easy, since travelling to other planets was not yet possible.

I **UNDERSTAND** THAT YOU WANT TO AVOID HUMANS FOR A WHILE. BUT DO YOU **REALLY** HAVE TO TRAVEL TO SPACE TO DO THAT? CAN'T YOU MAYBE MOVE TO THE **JUNGLE** OR THE **NORTH POLE** OR THE **DESERT** OR SOMETHING? OR JUST TO A CABIN IN THE **WOODS**?

He's right, of course. It *would* be simpler to just go and live somewhere on Earth where humans don't go. Jane Goodall lived in the jungle of Tanzania with chimps for many years in order to study them. I could do something like that.

OLGA, THE GIRL WHO LIVED WITH **WOLVES**
(COOLNESS SCORE: 1000)

OLGA, THE GIRL WHO LIVED WITH **SQUIRRELS**
(COOLNESS SCORE: LOWER)

OLGA, THE GIRL WHO LIVED WITH **FROGS**
(COOLNESS SCORE: 0
DISCOMFORT SCORE: 1000)

That's all pretty tempting (well, maybe not the frogs), but I'm not ready to give up the idea of travelling to space. For one thing, I would like to be a pioneer. And also, the whole point is to get to meet Meh's family, or other cool aliens like her.

Chuck understood, although he said that if he travelled to outer space, he would feel lonely out there—even with a pack of Olgamuses. I don't know. I guess I might, too. But there's no way to know until I try, right?

82

Chuck got up and went to the sink. He said hi to Rita, my spider. He likes her, and I suspect that Rita has a crush on Chuck. She always bats her eight eyes when he talks to her.

BONJOUR, CHÈRE RITA!

BONJOUR, CHER CHUCK.

OBSERVATION #9:

CHUCK'S FRENCH IS WAY BETTER THAN MINE.

"Hey," Chuck said. "What will you do with your spider if you move to another planet?"

I told him that I needed to look up whether bugs can go into space. Chuck was curious as well, so we looked it up on the internet.

Well, it turns out that many bugs have space travelled! Apparently, NASA likes to send all sorts of living creatures into space. Look at this:

SPACE-TRAVELLING BUGS IN HISTORY:

FRUIT FLIES! IN 2006, NASA SENT 15 FRUIT FLIES INTO ORBIT, AND THE SPACE SHUTTLE CAME BACK TWO WEEKS LATER WITH 3,000 FRUIT FLIES ON BOARD.

SILKWORMS! THEIR EGGS AND LARVAE HAVE TRAVELLED IN SPACE FOR DECADES.

ANTS! NASA SENT 800 OF THEM TO THE INTERNATIONAL SPACE STATION TO SEE IF THEIR BEHAVIOUR WOULD CHANGE IN SPACE.

WE DID IT!

HONEYBEES! NASA SENT 3,500 OF THEM INTO ORBIT IN 1984 AND DISCOVERED THAT THE BEES WERE ABLE TO BUILD NESTS IN SPACE JUST LIKE THEY DO ON EARTH!

SPIDERS! YES, SPIDERS HAVE SUCCESSFULLY TRAVELLED IN SPACE. AND GUESS WHAT? THEIR WEBS WERE A BIT WOBBLY AT FIRST, BUT THEY LEARNED TO BUILD GOOD ONES AFTER A WHILE!

Isn't that great? I rushed to hug Rita, but of course, I couldn't—it would kill her. So I just blew her a kiss, which made her web wobble.

"Did you hear that, Rita? You can come to space with me and Meh!" Rita seemed totally thrilled. She swung a bit from her thread and smiled.

I was dancing around on the carpet when I stepped on something wet. Mister had peed everywhere, as was his speciality.

"Oops," said Chuck. "I guess Mister needs to go to the park. Wanna come and play some Frisbee?"

EWW!

7

BAD FRISBEE & SOME WORRIES

After I cleaned up the pee on my rug (YAY! my favourite activity!), I tried to put Meh's lead on and take her to the park. But she still wouldn't budge!

"Come on, Meh! It's a gorgeous day outside. Fresh air will do you good!"

*NOPE.

OBSERVATION # 10:

THE BRAKES ON THAT CREATURE ARE PRETTY EFFICIENT.

But no, nothing would convince her. So finally I put her in my backpack and off we went.

Mister was pretty frantic. He LOVES Frisbee. I sat Meh on a park bench so she could watch us. Apparently my Frisbee technique is something special, and Chuck wouldn't stop laughing.

OBSERVATION # 11:

PLAYING FRISBEE
IS HARDER THAN IT SEEMS.

We played for a while, and then we were interrupted by a horrible sound—a cry of disgust.

It was the Lalas. Well, it turned out that Meh had vomited on Farla's shoes.

"Your pet just puked on me!!!"

OBSERVATION # 12:

IF HAVING DIRTY SHOES IS "THE WORST THING EVER," YOUR LIFE IS PRETTY GOOD.

SORRY ABOUT THAT, BUT IF SMELLY SHOES COULD MAKE A PERSON DIE, THERE'D BE **NO HUMANS LEFT ON THIS EARTH.**

WHAT'S **WRONG** WITH MEH? MAN, DOES SHE **STINK!** DON'T YOU **EVER** WASH HER?

I **JUST DID!** MAYBE IT'S YOUR UPPER LIP THAT STINKS!

But it was true. Meh was very smelly, even after her bath.

"And what are those disgusting things on her tummy?"

I looked closely at Meh's belly and I saw pink pimples I hadn't noticed. Lots of them. It looked awful.

FIG. 6:

THE WEIRD WELTS

Meh was very sick. I had to take her home. I delicately put her in my backpack and said, "Sorry again about your shoes," to Farla.

Chuck and Mister came with me. We put Meh to sleep in her rubbish bin, and I took her temperature, only to realize that I have no idea what an Olgamus's normal temperature is like, so there was no way to know if she had a fever.

She did feel hot to the touch. I was so scared.

8

ALIEN DISEASES

Chuck stayed with us all evening, helping me take care of poor, sick Meh.

We offered her water, wiped her fur with a wet flannel, covered her with warm blankets, and turned the lights off in my bedroom. I played her one of my best ukulele lullabies, and she drifted off to sleep.

I was the **BEST NURSE EVER.**

The problem was that we have no idea what diseases affect alien creatures. Maybe they are similar to ours, but maybe not.

"Maybe we should go to the library and look up animal diseases," Chuck suggested. "Since Meh looks a bit like a pig, maybe she could have some kind of pig infection."

IT'S TRUE: THEY ARE SIMILAR.

That was a good idea, but I couldn't stand leaving Meh alone in her sad state. Chuck agreed to stay at my house to "babysit" while I went on my errand.

Ms Swoop wasn't at the library today; instead, it was the horrible Mr Gumstrap, the other librarian.

So I didn't ask for help. Instead I looked on the computer for books about animal diseases. There weren't any. There were lots of books like this:

Hmmm, yeah. Maybe the adult section would be more help. I love to go there. It's quiet and it makes me feel all grown up.

Unfortunately, there wasn't anything useful to me in that section either. The only book about diseases was this:

I'm pretty certain Meh's not a plant.

I went back home and found Chuck reading comic books on the sofa.

SO, WHAT DID YOU LEARN?

I googled **"ALIEN DISEASES."**

Here are some of the frightening entries that we got:

OK, that's not exactly what I was looking for.

OBSERVATION # 13:

THE INTERNET IS NOT THE BEST PLACE TO
GO IF YOU'RE LOOKING FOR REASSURANCE.

"Hmm," I said.

Maybe a normal vet would do the trick. I looked at Meh, who was snoring in her rubbish bin. If she was still sick tomorrow, I'd take her to the vet.

9

DR SPIFFLE

That night, I put Meh's rubbish bin right next to my bed, where I could keep an eye on her and help if there was a problem. She slept through the night, and in the morning, she seemed better.

She got up, ate a full bowl of olives as usual, and drank some water. She looked a bit bloated and seemed full of gas. Also, her farts smelled terrible, but that's normal for her so I wasn't too worried.

STINK LEVEL:

NORMAL.

I was examining the spots on her tummy, which were still there, when something horrifying happened:

She had never done that before! That's when I knew there was something very, very wrong with my beloved Olgamus.

It hurt. I have to remind you that her fangs are pretty sharp, like a cat's. Now I had two deep holes in the side of my hand, and I felt like crying.

WAS SHE TURNING INTO A

WERE-OLGAMUS?

Meh looked at me with annoyed eyes and went back to her rubbish bin. And me? I washed my hand and worried that I might be infected with Meh's disease, so I used plenty of soap and water and a few plasters.

This was extremely worrying behaviour. It was not like her at all. She must have been in a lot of pain to bite the hand that feeds her.

There was no time to lose! I had to go to the vet. But which one? I turned on my computer and did a Google search for "special vet" in my neighbourhood.

Here's the page that came up first:

DR SPIFFLE'S CLINIC

THE BEST VET IN THE UNIVERSE!

ON TOP OF BEING **HANDSOME, GLAMOROUS** AND **FAMOUS,** DR SPIFFLE WILL TAKE CARE OF YOUR BELOVED CREATURES, WHATEVER THEY ARE!

WE SPECIALIZE IN

EXOTIC PETS

| JOIN US | PHOTOS | TESTIMONIES | CONTA |

His web page was full of links to articles about him curing famous people's pets and pictures of him at veterinarian galas and conferences and everything. He was apparently the vet to Bip Bibop's turtle, Arsenia.

It was all a bit over the top, but I decided to go with him. Plus, his clinic was just a few streets away.

I called Chuck, who came to meet me with the pet carrier he uses when he has to transport Mister.

I didn't want Meh to bite me again, so I used my biggest oven gloves to transfer her into the carrier.

Meh didn't seem to agree with my plans. She started howling.

DOWOOWOO

Walking to the clinic with the carrier was no easy feat; she was getting HEAVY! And poor Meh howled the whole way, making people curious.

When we entered, there was a very chic waiting room with tons of pets already. We went to the reception desk, where a young woman named Karen welcomed us.

Karen bent over the counter to peer inside. She had big wide eyes, which opened even wider when Meh started howling again.

Karen told us to sit down while we waited for Dr Spiffle to call us. The waiting room was full, and everybody was watching us:

THIS LADY WITH AN EXTREMELY **OBESE CAT**

THIS OLD WOMAN WITH **A SLEEPING SNAKE**

THIS TINY GUY WITH **A GIANT DOG**

THIS VERY
TOUGH-LOOKING PUNK
WITH A CUTE FLUFFY
BUNNY

THIS LITTLE BOY WITH A
BORED GUINEA PIG

THIS ANCIENT MAN WITH A
WEIRD-LOOKING PARROT

Everybody in the room loved animals, just like me,
and after a while I started feeling like these people
were my friends. We talked about our best friends.
We started talking about our pets' feats of brilliance
and funny habits.

Here's what our animal companions could do:

PET FEATS

PUDDING THE DOG COULD PLAY VIDEO GAMES WITH HIS **SNOUT** ON THE TABLET.

2 X 8 = 16

2 X 9 = 18

SPENCER THE PARROT HAD **MEMORIZED** ALL THE MULTIPLICATION TABLES FROM **ONE** TO **TWELVE.**

COWBOY THE BUNNY COULD EAT A 25-CENTIMETRE-LONG **CELERY** STICK IN **TWELVE** SECONDS.

CRUNCH CRUNCH

VLADIMIR THE CAT COULD RUN HERSELF A **BATH** (SHE WAS ONE OF THE VERY FEW CATS WHO LOVE BATHS).

BORIS THE GUINEA PIG COULD **OPEN** HIS OWN CAGE DOOR.

BERNARD THE SNAKE HAD NO PARTICULAR SKILL AND **NEVER** DID ANYTHING FUNNY.

SSSSSSSORRY!

After about fifty minutes, most animals had been seen by the vet and left. We were next. Meh had fallen asleep in my lap, and Chuck was reading one of the very fascinating magazines that were kept on a glass table. I was getting pretty bored when the door to the office opened. A man came out, holding a folder.

UH, EXCUSE ME, IS THERE A MEH? I'M **DR SPIFFLE.** PLEASE FOLLOW ME.

DR SPIFFLE

10

"PLEASE SIGN HERE"

The examination room was bare and cold, with sinister-looking tools, a bright lamp, ads about worms and fleas on the walls, and a row of jars containing liquids and pills.

Dr Spiffle looked more like a movie star than a vet. His white shirt was unbuttoned, and he was wearing a gold chain. He kept tossing his hair like a horse who's being bothered by buzzing flies.

FIG. 8: DR SPIFFLE

"So," Dr Spiffle said. "Karen tells me you have an unknown animal species. Let's take a look."

I didn't like the way Dr Spiffle was looking at Meh. He looked as if he were trying to figure out if Meh was edible.

MAGNIFICENT! HEH–HEH–HEH.

"Well," I said, "it's not an UNKNOWN. It's an *Olgamus ridiculus*. I discovered it and studied it and I actually know a lot about her."

"Really? Fascinating! Such a small girl, discovering a species. Heh-heh-heh."

What did he think was funny about a small girl discovering a species? Did all animal discoveries have to be made by tall old men? I was annoyed.

Dr Spiffle picked up Meh and started turning her this way and that, looking at her from all angles. He probed his fingers in her mouth, which Meh HATES.

As soon as Dr Spiffle put Meh back on the table, she ran to hide inside her carrier. She was looking at me with sad, pitiful eyes. She looked like:

She didn't like Dr Spiffle, and to be frank, I didn't like him much either. He didn't take me seriously, and he acted like he knew my own pet better than I did. I felt like grabbing Meh and leaving, but I had to wait and see if he was going to be able to help us.

He took out a notebook and a pen and started asking me questions.

What did that have to do with curing Meh?

He asked a dozen more questions: what did she eat? Had she gained weight recently? Was she aggressive? Did she sleep a lot? What did her poo look like? Did she exercise?

I told him about the symptoms that were worrying me:

THE **VOMITING**

BLARGH

THE **PIMPLES**

THE **SLEEPINESS**

OW!

GNAP!

THE **BAD TEMPER** THAT MADE HER BITE ME FOR THE FIRST TIME

Dr Spiffle was still taking notes. After a while, he pulled Meh out of her carrier again and looked in her ears and at her behind, and he measured her. This was all new information that I hadn't thought of noting down:

FINDINGS:

MEH IS **45** CENTIMETRES LONG

SHE'S **25** CENTIMETRES TALL

AND HER WAIST CIRCUMFERENCE IS **75** CENTIMETRES.

"Do you think you can help her?" I asked him. "Will she be OK?"

"Well, sweetie, her symptoms are certainly worrying," said Dr Spiffle.

Sweetie. I hate that. Did he call his adult male customers SWEETIE? I don't think so.

I didn't like this idea at all. I didn't want to leave Meh alone here with this annoying man.

I'M NOT SURE. I'D RATHER TAKE HER HOME WITH ME. CAN'T YOU JUST, I DON'T KNOW, GIVE US SOME TIPS?

LOOK, KID, I'M AFRAID IF YOU DON'T LEAVE HER HERE WITH ME, THERE COULD BE GRAVE CONSEQUENCES. I HAVE EVERYTHING WE NEED TO CURE HER, BUT I NEED TO RUN SOME TESTS, LIKE X-RAYS, TO MAKE A DIAGNOSIS.

"Please sign here," he said. "Don't worry. You can trust me, sweetie. I'm the best vet on Earth."

 DR SPIFFLE'S VET CLINIC

I agree to leave my pet_____ in the care of Dr Spiffle's clinic. I hereby authorize Dr Spiffle to perform tests and experiments, take pictures, and gather information as to the nature of my pet's illness. I also authorize him to administer medication and perform surgery if necessary.

Sign Here:_____
Date:_____

He gave me a huge, bright, movie-star smile and pat-
ted my head. I HATE it when people pat my head. I
REALLY didn't like that man.

But what choice did I have? I wanted to do everything I possibly could to cure Meh.

I signed the paper.

I scratched Meh between the ears, in that spot she likes, but Dr Spiffle took me by the arm and gently pulled me out of the room. Meh was trembling at the back of her carrier, and my heart was breaking.

And then he pushed me out the door.

Chuck was waiting for me in the waiting room. I must have had a worried expression on my face, because he stood up and gave me a big giant hug.

I was so sorry to leave the vet's office without Meh. Just the way she looked at me as I left the room! Would she ever forgive me?

Chuck took my hand, and we walked out together. "Let's go get a snack at Mr Hoopah's shop," Chuck said. "My treat."

STUFF 'N' MO

AND WIGS! AND SHOES!

AND DOUGHNUTS!

AND T

COME IN
WE'RE
OPEN

WE HAVE
FAKE MOU
IN AMER

When Mr Hoopah saw my red eyes, he asked what was wrong. I told him about the vet, and he looked sad.

"I have a surprise for you, dear customer," he said. "Freeze-dried food is astronaut food. For your trip! Come back tomorrow—I ordered freeze-dried olives for your buddy."

Mr Hoopah also gave us mustard-flavoured dog biscuits for Mister. "The treats are on me. I hope our friend gets better soon!"

Mister was waiting for us in the back yard. He was so happy when he saw Chuck that he ran in three-dimensional circles.

I gave Mister a big hug and instantly felt a bit better.

OBSERVATION # 15:

HUGS FROM UGLY DOGS
HAVE MAGICAL PROPERTIES.

When they left, though, I instantly felt as lonely as if I'd been lost in space, all alone in a bubble. The house was so dark and so quiet without Meh. I missed her snoring and even her weird smell.

I tried to read a bit but I couldn't focus, so I sat on the porch to think. I could see the stars and the moon, and it made my problems seem a tiny bit smaller.

And yet I was still feeling terrible about leaving Meh at the clinic. There was something really strange about this Dr Spiffle, aside from being arrogant and treating me like a five-year-old. I felt a deep distrust towards this man. His fake smile, the way he rushed me to sign the form and then quickly shoved me out of the room. It all felt wrong.

OMG!

That's when it dawned on me.

DR SPIFFLE KIDNAPPED MEH!

He probably wanted to pretend that he had discovered the new species all by himself! And he looked like the kind of guy who would want his face in all the newspapers!

And what if he was even more evil than that? What if, like in the *E.T.* movie, he wanted to "run some tests" on poor Meh? He had made me sign that sinister paper!

Meh was a gentle, sweet creature! She trusted me, and I'd left her alone in an office with an evil man. I had to go back to the vet's and save her.

I looked at the time. It was 7:42. I had no idea if the clinic was closed yet, but I put my shoes on and ran, still wearing my pyjamas. There was no time to lose.

I'M COMING, MEH!

OBSERVATION # 16:

I RUN FASTER IN MY PYJAMAS.
GOOD TO KNOW IF I EVER RUN A MARATHON.

I ran as fast as I could, but when I got to the clinic, the door was locked. All the lights were off except for a room at the back. I heard flickers, camera shutters maybe. I started banging on the door like a maniac.

But nobody came. I kept hearing the sounds of a camera and then I heard Dr Spiffle's dorky laugh. I stuck my ear to the window and tried to listen. I thought I could hear a faint "dow-dow-dowd," but I couldn't be sure.

There was nothing I could do but wait until the morning. Before I left, I yelled:

BE BRAVE, MEH!
I'LL BE BACK!

Sadly, I walked back to my house and tried to sleep. But it was impossible. I was too stressed out. I had to do something. I had to keep moving. So I decided to pack for my space trip, whenever that might happen.

Here's what I put in my backpack:

MR HOOPAH'S
ASTRONAUT FOOD*
& WATER

A DOZEN
COMIC
BOOKS

MY UKULELE

OLIVES
(FOR MEH)

A PEN

MY PHONE
(FOR THE CAMERA)

*I wish I could leave tomorrow. I can't wait to try the freeze-dried ice cream!

And then at some point, I fell asleep, and I had this dream: I was in this space bubble with Meh, and we were floating over this strange planet, where some creatures were waiting for us. It was

BEAUTiFUL.

… And then of course, I woke up, and was back on Earth. A brutal reality. I had to go save my buddy. The clinic opened at nine a.m., but it was only seven. I decided to leave right away. Waiting at home would be torture.

12

THE

PHOTO SHOOT

When the clinic opened, I had been waiting on the doorstep for 45 minutes. A few other clients and their animals were waiting as well.

Karen was at the desk.

I was sorry I shouted at her, but I was very upset.

"I'm sorry, but Dr Spiffle is running some very important tests on your pet right now. Please calm down. I have strict instructions not to interrupt him while he's working," Karen explained.

This wouldn't do. I was hearing weird noises and laughter coming from Dr Spiffle's office. I decided to trust my instincts and go in. I took off and ran past Karen's desk towards the doctor's door.

"You can't go in there! Dr Spiffle is—"

I opened the office door quickly before Karen could stop me. I was prepared for almost anything, but not for this:

Dr Spiffle was in the middle of a photo shoot.

Dr Spiffle turned to look at me.

"What's happening in here?" I asked.

"I'm sorry, Doctor," said Karen. "I tried to stop her."

I ran to Meh and took her in my arms. She looked annoyed, but not hurt.

Dr Spiffle looked a little bit weird. He was chuckling as though the whole thing was just a funny misunderstanding.

"Your Instasnap account?" I said. "What's that?"

Then he took out his phone, opened an app, and showed me a lot of pictures of himself.

712 LIKES

DR SPIFFLE ON A BEACH RUNNING IN THE WAVES

821 LIKES

DR SPIFFLE ON TOP OF A MOUNTAIN, HAIR BLOWING IN THE WIND

612 LIKES

DR SPIFFLE ON AN ELEPHANT

160

DR SPIFFLE
EATING RAVIOLI

DR SPIFFLE
DRINKING A LATTE

"I'm a bit of an internet star," he explained. "In my spare time, I like to do some modelling, and I just thought that your, er, pet and I could make some great pictures."

I couldn't believe it. This sounded so unprofessional. At the same time, I was kind of relieved because I'd thought this guy was plain evil, when actually he just loved attention from strangers.

"Did you even try to cure her?" I asked. "Are you even a real doctor?"

"Oh, yes, yes, yes," he said. "Of course. Please calm down, sweetie. I ran plenty of tests. Here, I'll show you." He picked up a file on his desk and leafed through it.

NAME: MEH
SPECIES: OLGAMUS RIDICULUS

"OK," he said. "We can rule out an intestinal obstruction. Her temperature is stable. She doesn't look like she's in any pain, and the welts on her tummy are very possibly some form of acne. One thing I noticed is that her abdomen seems a bit bloated, but that might be due to gas. I wouldn't worry about it. She might be eating too much. I suggest limiting her calorie intake and more exercise."

"Oh," I said. "Uh, thanks, I guess."

"It's been a pleasure. And while we're at it, I made a couple of observations that might be of interest to you. I added them to her file. I'll ask Karen to make a copy for you."

A few moments later, Karen handed me this:

MEH
OLGAMUS RIDICULUS

TOOK BLOOD SAMPLE:
OLGAMUS BLOOD IS BRIGHT BLUE.

HER TAIL BONE SEEMS TO BE ELASTIC:
BENDABLE AND RETRACTABLE.

SHE HAS FLEAS.
(PLEASE ASK AT DESK FOR FLEA SHAMPOO.)

This file was surprisingly helpful. I folded it and placed it in my notebook.

"Thanks," I said again.

"I really am sorry about the photo shoot, dear. To make it up to you, I'd like to give you this visit and a bottle of flea shampoo for free."

I picked Meh up, put her in my backpack, and left.

I guess I was a bit harsh on the doctor. He wasn't really that bad. He just had weird internet hobbies. And I had to admit that Meh looked awfully cute in her unicorn outfit.

I took Meh home and examined her thoroughly, just in case. She had lost a bit of fur—that might have been caused by stress. She looked exhausted, so I tried to be as soothing as possible while examining her.

OBSERVATION # 17:

PHYSICAL APPEARANCE:
OTHER THAN THE WEIGHT, NORMAL

APPETITE:
NORMAL TO HIGH

ENERGY LEVEL:
LOW—BUT SHE MIGHT HAVE BEEN VERY TIRED FROM THE NIGHT AT THE VET'S

PINK BUMPS:
STILL THERE. HE HADN'T
CURED THOSE.

STINKINESS LEVEL:
NORMAL-HIGH

**PLAYFULNESS
LEVEL:**
NULL

**CUTENESS
LEVEL:**
HIGH, AS USUAL

169

After petting her and hugging her for a while, I sat her up in her rubbish bin, played her some ukulele songs, and let her sleep. She needed some rest.

13

PETFINDER iN ACTION

When I woke up a couple of hours later, she wasn't there any more.

No answer. I looked in my room, in the bathroom, in the kitchen: no sign of Meh. I looked under the bed, in the cupboard, under the sofa, and in every blanket.

The door to the house was closed and locked, so she couldn't have got out.

WHERE WAS SHE HIDING?

The doorbell rang again: it was Chuck.

Meh had a history of vanishing. This time I wasn't too worried, since, as I said, the front door was closed.

MEH IS TURNING ME INTO A PET DETECTIVE!

Meh is an adventurous napper. We had to look EVERY-
WHERE, even in the most improbable places.

STRANGE NAP SPOTS OF THE PAST:

THE
DIRTY LAUNDRY
BASKET

THE
RECYCLING
BIN

MY **UNDERWEAR** DRAWER

THE **BOTTOM** SHELF OF MY BOOKCASE

THE **SINK**

"Well," said Chuck, "she's a real champ at hide-and-seek. You can add that to your observations."

So I did. Here goes:

OBSERVATION # 18:

OLGAMUSES
ARE HIDE-AND-SEEK
CHAMPiONS

"Maybe she slipped out the door when you came in?" I said. "I can't think where to look next. It's like she vanished or evaporated."

Chuck and I stood there, not knowing what to do next, when the doorbell rang again.

It was the Lalas, all dressed up as doctors.

HEY, OLGA! WE WERE **WORRIED** ABOUT MEH. HOW IS SHE? WE CAME TO **HELP.**

"Thanks for the olives," I said. "Meh seems better, but unfortunately, I have no idea where she is. I was starting to think maybe she was with you guys."

"No, she's not," they said.

"OK, then come in. Maybe you can help me find her."

The Lalas looked a bit silly in their costumes, but I was glad they were here. I had a real search party helping me.

I'LL JUST PUT THE OLIVES IN THE FRIDGE, AND THEN WE CAN START **THE SEARCH.**

I went to the kitchen and opened the fridge door. On the bottom shelf, between a bunch of asparagus and a bowl of leftover mac and cheese, was Meh. She was surrounded by a pile of spring rolls.

"What are you doing in the fridge, Meh?" I asked. "And where did you find those spring rolls? I don't remember buying any!"

"Olga," said Chuck, "have you ever seen spring rolls that

14

SOME SPRING ROLLS

It was true. The spring rolls were moving. Squirming, to be more precise. And when I looked closely, I saw that they had little faces.

They were not spring rolls at all.

THEY WERE BABIES.

BABY OLGAMUSES!!!

O.M.G.

They were so ADORABLE!

That's why Meh had been acting all weird!

She was lying on her side, looking content. She was looking at us with sleepy eyes, blinking a little bit. She was emitting a weird noise I'd never heard before that sounded like a tin opener or a big electric toothbrush.

BZZZZR
BZZRRR

She was

PURRiNG.

She was

NURSiNG **HER**
BABiES!

I gently closed the fridge door to let her nurse in peace. Then Chuck and I sat down on the sofa and noted down everything that had happened with Meh so far.

MAJOR SCIENTIFIC EVENT!

OBSERVATION # 19:

1. THE **PINK BUMPS** WERE NIPPLES.

DUH.

I FEEL SO **STUPID** FOR NOT HAVING THOUGHT OF THAT!

2. SO OLGAMUSES ARE IN FACT **MAMMALS!**

3. BABY OLGAMUSES, LIKE SPRING ROLLS, ARE **BEST KEPT IN THE FRIDGE.**

SPRING ROLL = BABY OLGAMUS

4. THEIR BODIES ARE **SLIGHTLY TRANSLUCENT,** LIKE ... SPRING ROLLS.

5. THEY ARE MUCH MUCH **CUTER** THAN SPRING ROLLS, ALTHOUGH MAYBE NOT AS DELICIOUS.

PLEASE DO NOT EAT US!

Then I had a thought.

CHUCK! YOU KNOW **WHAT THIS MEANS, RIGHT?**

WHAT?

IT MEANS THAT THERE MUST BE A **MALE** OLGAMUS **SOMEWHERE** ON EARTH!

NOT NECESSARILY. SHE MIGHT HAVE BECOME PREGNANT BEFORE SHE LEFT HER PLANET. OR WHO KNOWS? MAYBE OLGAMUSES **DON'T** NEED A PARTNER TO MAKE BABIES.

HMM. YOU MIGHT BE RIGHT. I WAS GETTING MY HOPES UP. BUT IN ANY CASE, WE NOW HAVE AT LEAST **EIGHT OLGAMUSES** ON EARTH.

EIGHT OLGAMUSES. That's a lot more than we had before. That meant that the Earth, and specifically my fridge, now contained eight good reasons for me to stay here.

These babies were not ready for a trip yet.

It was time to celebrate. Chuck and I went to Mr Hoopah's shop to get some ice cream and some fancy olives for the new mum.

Oh, and another notebook too. I'm almost out of pages in this one, and with the new babies, there will be lots of

OBSERViNG TO DO.

Collect all of
OLGA and MEH's
SCIENTIFIC ADVENTURES

WALKER BOOKS

www.walker.co.uk